The Night Before Baseball at the Park by the Bay

To Coach Sara and our Ace Ryan - D.S.

For Aymone & Ali - M.P.

www.NightBeforeBaseball.com

Book design by Randall Heath

Special thanks to Mela Bolinao, Tim Travaglini, Emma D. Dryden, Jan Constantine, Jeff Bleich, Michael Manson, Audra Johnson and Alex Barkas (in memoriam)

Printed In USA

ISBN 978-0-9891043-0-2

5 7 9 10 8 6 4

The Night Before Baseball at the Park by the Bay

By
David
Schnell

Illustrated by
Macky
Pamintuan

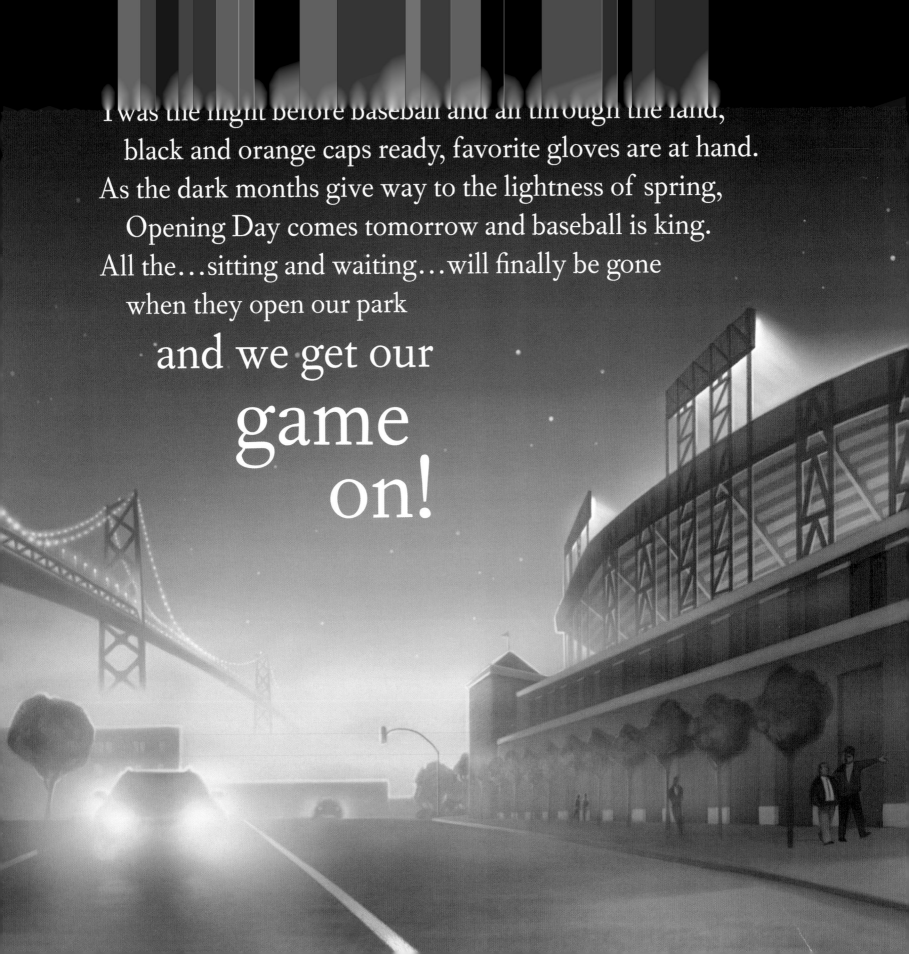

'Twas the night before baseball and all through the land,
black and orange caps ready, favorite gloves are at hand.
As the dark months give way to the lightness of spring,
Opening Day comes tomorrow and baseball is king.
All the…sitting and waiting…will finally be gone
when they open our park

and we get our

game
on!

In the shadows of dreams of the young boy this night,
   there is so much excitement and too much delight.
With the new season's start just hours away,
   he can't seem to rest, he just wants to play.
So he tosses and turns and imagines the joy
   of being a major league pitcher who is still just a boy.

While he falls deep asleep, Ryan cradles his glove
  and dreams of pitching a big game for the Giants, his love.
He has a sinker, a fastball, a change-up, a slurve.
  But most important of all, he has guts and the nerve
to pitch when most needed with courage and verve.

A dream team of Giants joins Ryan to play
   as they battle their rivals this Opening Day.
With Buster to catch, Matt and Timmy cheer on,
   fans are thrilled by the talent, the speed, and the brawn.
The crowd's all decked out in orange and black,
   they cheer and they scream, so glad to be back!

With the score tied at one, the pitching's been great.
  It's a duel among aces as the innings get late.
Each of these teams can still win the game.
  Both have sluggers galore that are too rough to tame.

They hit for the gaps and aim for the fences,
  work every at-bat to break down defenses.
In the bottom of the eighth, the Giants score a big run—
  to the last inning now, time to get the job done.

The Giants next pitcher controls the game's fate
  with the heart of the order due up at the plate.
In the lead by one run after eight innings played,
  the starter pitched swell, and he now needs some aid.

So Coach calls on young Ryan to finish the game
  as the ninth inning pitcher, the "Closer" by name.
Ryan's practiced a lifetime for this very chance
  to pitch the big game and make the ball dance.

Fans roar with excitement and shout out with glee,
as Ryan enters his first game at the park by the sea.
He jogs from the dugout surveying the crowd,
heart pumping intensely and thumping out loud.
His teammates cheer on as the players prepare,
but the other team taunts him as they stare and they glare.

The ump calls for the pitch. The crowd settles in.
The *first* batter leans in with a sneer and a grin.
Ryan steps on the mound, firmly gripping the ball.
Then he fires his best stuff, amazing them all.

The batter stands frozen,
dazed and confused—
fooled by three strikes,
his bat's never used.

With pitches so speedy and tricky and smart,
the *second* batter swings away right from the start.
Ryan's fastballs have zip, his curveballs have grooves,
the sliders he throws make incredible moves.

The batter takes aim and gives it his all.
    But try as he may, he can't hit the ball.
Ryan's skills on the mound seem well beyond doubt,
    as he paints the strike zone and the batter strikes out.

But the *third* batter, Brute, is the toughest of all.
  Pitchers fear him the most, he's crushed many a ball.
Home runs are his weapons each time he appears.
  One swing of his bat can bring pitchers to tears.
Brute is seasoned and salty and eats rookies for lunch.
  But young Ryan is crafty—and plays on a hunch.

Ryan pitches to full count. Brute puffs up at the plate.
  Brute's expecting a fastball, all speedy and straight.
Ryan fakes fastball motion BUT throws his best *slurve*—
  striking out the big Brute with a steely reserve!

Brute tosses his bat—he's been *fooled* by a kid?
  Then he nods to the mound;
with respect, tips his lid.

With three batters out, the Giants have won!
Fans erupt in great cheers for what Ryan has done.
He tosses his hat, his glove, and the ball,
then he pumps up his fist in front of them all.
Carried high by his teammates all calling his name,
Ryan shouts to the crowd,

"I love this game!"

As the morning sun rises and the boy starts to stir,
he awakes from his dream and at first it's a blur.
Then a smile appears, then a grin, then a laugh,
for last night was great fun, but it's only half

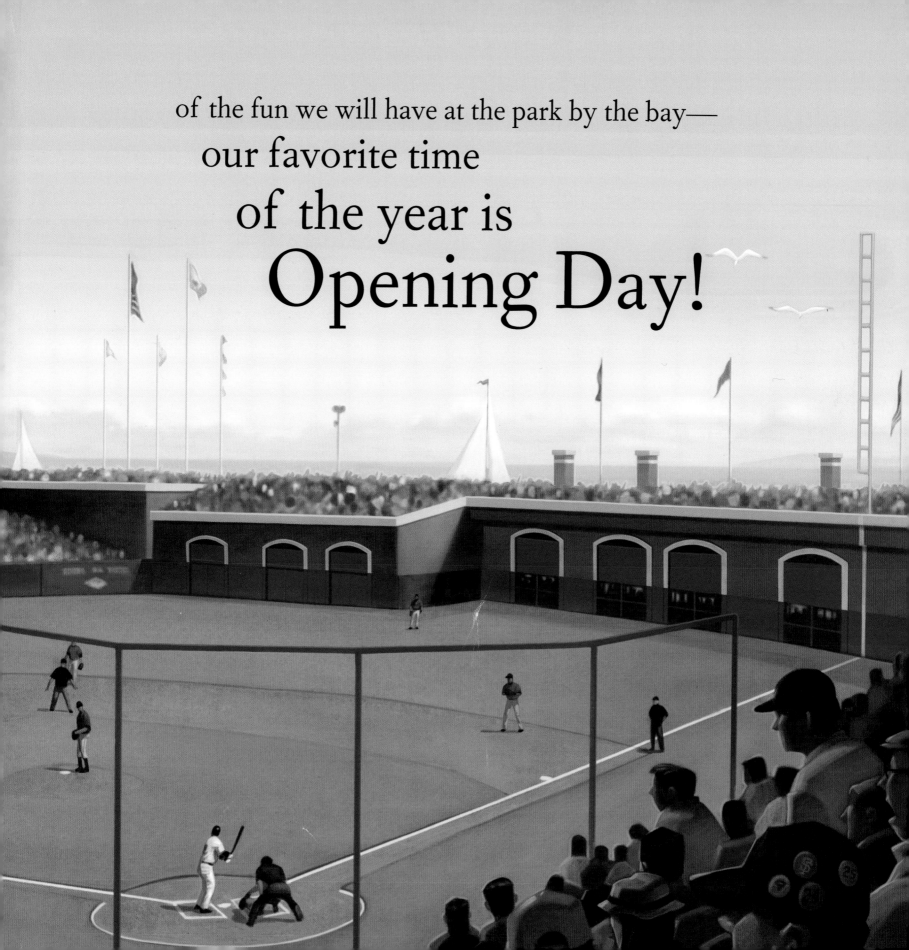

of the fun we will have at the park by the bay—
our favorite time
of the year is
Opening Day!

Hurray!

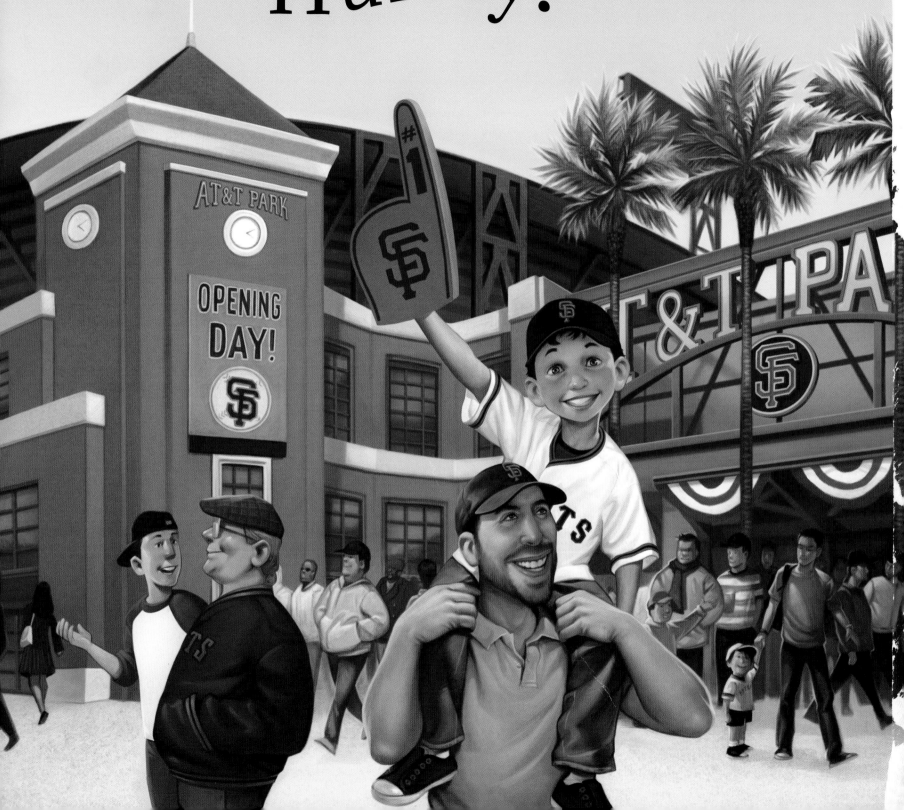